D0603802

[redacted] Library
[redacted] 0262975946

by Anna Kang *illustrated by* Christopher Weyant

We Are (Not) Friends

To Andrea, Ilene, Lisa, and Liz.
Thank you for all the fun playdates and belly laughs,
from childhood to adulthood—A. K.

To Tom, for a lifetime of friendship and laughs—C. W.

Text copyright © 2019 by Anna Kang
Illustrations copyright © 2019 by Christopher Weyant
All rights reserved. No part of this book may be reproduced, or stored in a retrieval system, or transmitted in any form or by any means, electronic, mechanical, photocopying, recording, or otherwise, without express written permission of the publisher.
Published by Two Lions, New York
www.apub.com
Amazon, the Amazon logo, and Two Lions are trademarks of Amazon.com, Inc., or its affiliates.
ISBN-13: 9781542044288 (hardcover) ISBN-10: 1542044286 (hardcover)
Design by Abby Dening
The illustrations are rendered in ink and watercolor with brush pens on Arches paper.
Printed in China | First edition
1 3 5 7 9 10 8 6 4 2

NORTHERN PLAINS
PUBLIC LIBRARY
Ault, Colorado

Can I play with you?

Yes!
Well . . .
Thanks!
BOING
BOING

NORTHERN PLAINS
PUBLIC LIBRARY
Ault, Colorado

TAPPA
TAPPA
TAPPITY
TAPPITY

BONK!

My hat!
WOOOSH
What? It was getting hot.
WHIRRRRRRRR

Let's play dinosaur hunters!

Where's our friend?
Who?

Our
friend—

We are friends.

We are *not*
friends with—

NORTHERN PL
PUBLIC LIBRARY
Ault, Colorado

I'm back!
Great! Now we *all* can play dinosaur hunters!
Great.
BOING

HEE! HEE! HEE!
HAW! HAW! HAW!

I know!
We can
build
a car!
A
jeep!

Great minds . . .
. . . think alike!

WHAP!
STACK! STACK!

BEEP!
BEEP!

SQUEAK!
OOOPH!
ERGG!!
Um . . .
it's a two-seater.
Then where do *I* sit?

You can be the dinosaur!
Yeah! Attack, T. rex!
Roar.

LOUDER!

ROAR!

SCARIER!

ROAR!!!

WHUMP!!!

WE ARE NOT

FRIENDS!!!

SNIFF!

You are right.
We are not friends.
We are *best* friends.

And this is our *new* friend?
Yes.

Yay! Do you want to play spies?
Yeah!

Can I
play too?